VAMPIRE D

Brian Grossman

Good Old Days Publishing

D

Life's too short.

So many times, he had heard that saying. *Life's too short not to take a chance on the girl next to you at the bar. Life's too short to hold onto a grudge. Life's too short to dress like shit on a Saturday night. Take a risk. Use the fine china.* All that bullshit.

So here he was. His name was D, and he had taken more risks than he could remember now. He was dressed up this Saturday evening; dressed up for the live jazz music in this downtown bar, anyway. He owned only fine china, and he couldn't help noticing that when he caught the eye of a young woman across the bar that she held his gaze for a moment. She was with a brawny jock who was clearly out of his element, but what the hell.

Life's too short.

He stepped outside and ran his fingers through his dark hair. Tilting his head back, he took in a deep breath of cool night air and smelled a thousand distinct scents. He reached into his vest pocket for his cigarette case, and then thought better of it. He had particularly bad smoker's breath after smoking this new batch.

He stepped back inside and walked over near the table where the girl was sitting with her date. The silence spoke volumes between short, shallow questions and short, uncomfortable answers. Blind date then. Luckily for D, the big guy decided to make the silence less awkward by taking a bathroom break. He smiled and sat down in the newly vacant seat.

"Work friend?" D asked.

"Excuse me?" she asked back.

"Was it a friend from work that set the two of you up? Or school, maybe?"

"Ahh," she smiled. "What makes you think this is our first time out together?"

"Oh, I could be completely off, of course. You two have brilliant chemistry." He smiled dryly. "Just judging by the venue that this was your choice, not his. He seems like the type who's used to getting his way."

She smiled. "So you picked up on that too, huh? Fine, you win. It was my friend Amy from work who set us up, supposedly to ease me back into the market." She laughed and brushed a lock of her red hair behind her ear. "I'm Shannon."

"I'm D." he replied.

"Now there's a name you don't hear every day," she said, sipping her wine. "What's it stand for?"

"Tonight? Nothing." He said with a smile.

"The mysterious stranger angle, not very original," she shook her head.

"Any more original than the tough guy with a soft side angle? I'll bet I play my role better."

"I guess we'll have to see." She gave a coy smile.

"I guess so."

Up front, the band eased into a new number. The bass player walked his hand up and down his instrument while the guitarist played over the top. Effortless scales with no wrong notes, sitting just long enough on each to create the feeling of anticipation that D loved jazz for.

"So Shannon, you were set up here by Amy from work. Where is work, exactly?"

There was a short pause while the trumpet held a trembling note before dancing back into harmony with the rest of the band.

"Dos Burritos over on Park," she said. "Front of house manager."

He could hear the slight quickening of her pulse in the words and knew the lie, smiling and nodding anyway. He'd gotten better at sensing them over time, and Shannon did not seem to be particularly good at concealing hers. D didn't mind it when people wove their untruths though, not for the most part. They were often interesting, and the imaginative ones deserved their due respect. Not this one, though. He let it slide.

"A nice place," he replied. "Been awhile since I was there. Now maybe I'll have a better reason to stop by."

She rolled her eyes but kept her smile. "And how about you?"

"Oh, this and that. Enough to keep busy."

"Still sticking with the mysterious stranger bit? Points for commitment I guess."

"Have to keep the nights interesting somehow."

"And how about tonight?" she asked. "Planning to steal me away and save me from my awful date?"

"Maybe, maybe not," replied D thoughtfully. "You stayed here this long, which means part of you likes a bad boy. Then again, if that's the case I can play along too"

A heavy tap on his shoulder punctuated his sentence for him. D turned and looked up a surprising distance to the man looming over him. He wore a bristly goatee on his face, along with a scowl.

"'Scuse me." He said gruffly. "That's my seat."

"Is it?" D raised an eyebrow. "Sorry, I saw you talking with the blonde bartender for a while and thought it was open. My mistake."

"I was n-..." the bug guy stuttered, fuming.

"No, no, it's ok," D soothed with a wink. "Guy like you needs options, especially on a blind date. No harm no foul, except maybe against Shannon."

"Shut up and get the fuck out outta my seat!" A thick arm grabbed D by the shoulder and hauled him roughly up and out of the chair. A faded "88" tattoo by his shoulder slipped into view from under the sleeve. On the stage behind, the music stepped up in pace and key. D recovered as gracefully as he could and brushed off his jacket.

"Can you believe this asshole?" the broad-shouldered man jerked a meaty thumb at D as he looked at Shannon incredulously.

"I dunno, Jay," she said carefully, clearly not wanting to get on his bad side.

This was where D was going to have to be careful. The girl was attractive, that was for sure. But was she worth it? He always kept as low a profile as he could when he went out in order to avoid trouble of any kind. Especially this kind.

However, that got boring after a while.

"Jay, is it? Tell you what, Jay. I'm gonna go around back and have a cigarette, but before that I wanted to say I recognize your ink. That's a prison tattoo and that gang it belongs to is known for being rapists in and out of the pen. Not sure how far your taste for bad boys goes, Shannon, just make sure you're ready for a couple bruises and a trip to the doctor to deal with whatever else he gives you."

There was stunned silence at the small table. Shannon's eyes were saucers, and Jay's face turned progressively darker shades of red as he readied himself to jump at D.

"Now for that cigarette! Thanks for your time." He said with a smile as he turned and strode to the back door. He listened carefully to the sound of Jay's chair scraping backwards, urgent whispers from Shannon, and the sound of his footfalls as he followed.

Pushing open the door, D walked past the patio and around the side of the building toward the back. The door slammed behind as Jay threw it shut. Luckily, there was only one other person outside smoking, and they were on their way back in. There would be nobody around behind the establishment.

"Hey!" shouted Jay as he caught up to D. "Who the fuck do you think you are? Saying that shit to me in front of my girl. You're gonna regret it bro, I'll fuck you up!"

The big man pulled back his arm and unleashed a giant haymaker with all of his weight and power behind it. If it connected, it would probably fold any man in one hit, and it looked like it had indeed worked many times before for this "Jay".

D spun to face his attacker and grabbed the offending fist an inch from his face. Clutching the man's wrist in a white-knuckled grip, he twisted into an arm lock and forced Jay to the ground. The big man hardly had time to blink in confusion before his face scraped the pavement.

D looked around. There were no cameras and no people around. The dumpsters at the corner of the building provided decent cover. Jay maneuvered his head up to look at the smaller man who had taken him down.

"What the fuck are you man, a black belt?" Really? What a dumb thing to say.

D decided to show him exactly what he was.

Wordlessly, his smile widened. He slowly squeezed his grip tighter on Jay's wrist until there came the muted pop of snapping bone. The big man cried out in pain, but D put a hand over his mouth. He stared hard at Jay until he locked eyes with him and saw the fear blossom. D's eyes remained passively amused, but their color changed. His irises rippled from dark brown to a pale gold that seemed to shimmer in the dim light.

As Jay's muffled protests became more and more frantic, D opened his mouth. It seemed that his entire bone structure was changing. His canines pushed farther and farther out, like two sabers being drawn from their sheaths. He pushed Jay's head away and sank his fangs into the man's jugular. His victim's eyes went wide and then rolled back in delirium.

After he was finished, D checked himself. He hadn't spilled; his shirt and jacket were still clean, and his victim was regrettably still alive. He wouldn't remember anything from the past hour or so, D had made sure. He missed the days when you could just dump a body and have that be the end of it. Ah well. Curse of the information age.

He propped Jay's prone form against the back face of the

farthest dumpster, popped a mint into his mouth and headed back inside. He'd let dinner settle and worry about dessert shortly.

Back at the table, Shannon was waiting with wide-eyed worry.

"What happened?" she asked. "Are you ok? Is he?"

"Of course!" D replied casually. "Just a little misunderstanding is all. We worked it out and everything's fine." He winked.

From her smell and the sound of her pulse, she didn't fully believe him but was glad enough to be rid of her blind date. Good enough.

"Anyway," he continued. "Let's get out of here. I know a couple places we can go. Jazz is a nice way to start out the evening, but the night is young and life's too short."

Too short for some, at any rate.

* * *

It was almost light out as D pulled up the driveway and into the garage. He waited patiently while the door lowered itself completely before getting out, as he always did. Better to be safe than sorry, especially after a night out hunting. He pulled off the license plates and tossed them on a workbench with a few others and unlocked the door.

The first thing he noticed was that the TV was on. Loud.

The second thing was the smell of smoke. Not current, but definitely very recent. His eyes flitted around the kitchen as he strode through it and down the hall. Water was running behind the third door on the left. He braced himself, pushed out his fangs, and threw the door open with a loud snarl.

A woman was inside the bathroom, covered in a towel and brushing her teeth. On the vampire's surprise attack, she gasped and stumbled backwards, arms flailing and toothbrush flying.

"JESUS CHRIST, D, WHAT THE FUCK?!?!" She screamed, gathering the towel that had come decidedly loose in her panic.

The vampire laughed and reached out a hand to help her up.

"Sorry Trace, couldn't resist. The hell are you doing up so

early, anyway?"

She slapped his hand away and crawled over to where her toothbrush lay by the bathtub, clearly not ready to forgive yet.

"I always get up early when you go out, just in case. And to make sure you didn't pop up on the news." That explained the volume on the TV.

"Well thank you darlin, I really appreciate it," he said. He was genuinely touched, but played the comment off as whimsical. He took the toothbrush and rinsed it for her. "Mind telling me why the house smells like burnt hair?"

"Just the kitchen," she said, though it was hard to understand because she was brushing her teeth again. "The wok wouldn't work right and I put too much oil in when I tried to fix it."

"Yeah, they don't get hot enough on regular stoves; I'll have to get a special burner for it. Nice try, Paula Deen."

"Screw you," she retorted, spitting into the sink and trying to hide her smile. She walked out of the bathroom and across the hall to her bedroom, shutting the door in D's face as he made to follow. "I'm glad you're home, though," She called through the closed door. "How'd it go?"

"Oh, fine," he said, leaning on the doorframe. "Met a nice girl, took her to a show, went out to a bar, showed her my car, dropped her off home. Very pleasant evening."

"Liar," she called. "I smell her on your clothes and breath. Did you hurt her?" She asked pointedly.

"No. Honestly. She did taste like she was close to having pre-diabetes, though."

The door opened and Tracy emerged fully clothed. Her damp blond hair hung loose about her shoulders as she looked him up and down.

"Say 'ah'," she commanded.

"Ahh," he said, rolling his eyes.

She sniffed his breath and wrinkled her nose. "You swear she's ok?"

"Promise. Public place, someone found her within minutes."

She gave him a light slap on the cheek and walked back to the kitchen.

"I don't know why you'd wanna go out for burgers when there's steak waiting for you at home," she said over her shoulder.

"What, the same steak I have every night?" He teased. "Also, burgers don't have a jealous boyfriend. Blood isn't my only need, you know."

"Riiight," she said, scrubbing the wok in the sink.

"How is Marky-Mark anyhow?" asked D.

"*Matt* is fine, thanks. And thanks for the night off. It's getting late, you'd better get down there. Nightcap?"

"I'm good, thanks. Daycap?" He smiled.

"Maybe. I think I'll do some sculpting today, it might be nice."

"Come on then, you'll have to tuck me in for it." He winked and opened the cellar door. She shook her head and walked down after him.

The Blood Bond is a curious thing. Ordinarily, vampires feed on human blood and not vice versa. A gift of blood can be given to a human, however, bestowing certain enhancing properties as well as a slight sense of euphoria. Once the human receives this gift ten or so times, a very deep and lasting attachment is formed.

D had had many Familiars through the Blood Bond over the years, each different and always invaluable. Many took care of his baser needs, others took care of much more. All watched over him during the day and were constant companions. The cool and callous demeanor that D had developed over the years melted with them and the attachment was real in both directions, a rarity in the vampire circles.

Tracy was by far his favorite Familiar yet. She was in her late twenties, unmarried and spirited. An accomplished artist, she could work from home without any difficulty. The Bond reinforced her maternal instincts toward D, so while there was some element of infatuation, their relationship had remained almost playfully platonic.

Being an artist also allowed Tracy a certain amount of

leeway when buying eccentric items such as the coffin in the basement, as she could always allude to working on a new project if asked directly by curious outsiders. A coffin was certainly not necessary in the modern world of heavy curtains and hermetically sealed rooms, but D liked the familiarity and comfort. He opened the lid and hopped inside.

"If you need anything, yell or something." D said as he rolled back a cuff on his sleeve and poked it with a fang.

"Right," she countered. "Through the basement door, down the stairs, and through the sealed room and cushy coffin lid. I'll yell all right. You should put a radio or walkie in here like I asked you to do months ago."

She took his offered wrist before the thin blood could trickle down his arm and appeared to give it a long kiss. Wiping her mouth, she gave D a peck on the cheek and closed the lid.

"Have a good day," he said.

"You too."

***

Back upstairs, Tracy unwrapped a few blocks of clay and sat on the floor in front of the TV. With a couple sculpting tools strewn around her crossed legs, she probingly shaped the clay and intermittently changed channels. Lost in thought, she almost missed her phone ringing.

"Hello?"

"Hey there, I thought you might be up." Matt sometimes called on his way to work in the mornings, particularly when traffic was locked up.

"Hi, g'morning! How's traffic today?"

"Lousy. You think three lanes would be enough, but apparently not. Gives me more time with you anyway. I missed you last night," He added.

"I missed you too. How did everything go?

"It was great!" Matt exclaimed. "I took the lead and talked up our clients at dinner, and they were totally sold on us!"

"That's great!" Tracy joined in. "And they were worried about you having no experience in sales."

"Thanks babe. I have a follow-up meeting with the new boss this morning, hopefully it'll be more good news."

"That's terrific! Hope it goes well!"

"Thanks. I still feel bad that this dinner had to be on your one night off for the week."

"That's ok," Tracy said. "That's just how it is sometimes. We can deal."

"I'll make it up to you, I promise. Dinner out at the new steakhouse downtown as soon as we're both free for a night."

"I'd love it." Tracy smiled. "I miss you."

"I miss you too, babe. You know, if things work out for me in this new position, maybe we can finally move in together. I know the old guy you take care of is gonna miss you, but maybe you can drop down to part time."

Tracy laughed lightly. "We'll cross that bridge when we get there I guess. For now, it's a good arrangement that works out for everyone. Tell you what, though: When I move next, I want it to be with you."

***

Tracy put her music back on and keyed up the Red Hot Chili Peppers to get her back into the sculpting groove. She turned it up and left the news channel going on the television as well. She really liked the way her clay was shaping up, and concentrated hard to keep the mood of the piece consistent.

She may have heard the crack at the door if any one of these factors was different, but then again maybe not. From the back kitchen door there came another crack and a groan, and the door quietly opened. In its frame was a hydraulic tool that stretched across the opening. A gloved hand pushed a release button and the piston closed itself.

The intruder stepped gingerly into the kitchen and took in his surroundings. He heard the most noise coming from the adjacent room. His eyes flitted about, assessing the implements and wares around him. He pulled a butcher knife quietly from the knife block, turned it over in his hand, and put it back. From his pocket he extracted a bulky folding blade and held it closed in his fist and peered around the corner.

A girl was sitting on the hardwood floor in front of the TV with an indeterminate shape of clay in front of her, facing away from him. The only hallway was just beyond her. There was no other way.

He stalked into the living room and slowly inched his way up to the seated figure in front of him. She was humming a tune and whittling away at what appeared to be a humanoid tree made of dark clay. Maybe he could simply strike her unconscious and deal with her later.

No. There were two things he came for and if he didn't get at least one, then...he needed to get at least one. Better to start right away. He slowly opened the folding knife in his hand, a matte serrated blade with undulating grooves along its surface. Slowly, he thumbed it open as he raised his hand, *clicking* it locked only as he swung the blade down towards the girl's neck.

***

That click Tracy heard.

The fear and surprise brought a rush of adrenaline flowing through her veins. In most people, this would cause a momentary freeze of sorts, similar to the "deer in the headlights" effect. That half-second of paralytic panic was her death sentence.

Luckily, Tracy was not most people.

Her fear and panic translated into a piercing gasp as she vaulted herself to the side and slashed out with her sculpting knife. The arcing strike that was meant to sever her neck to the spine instead lacerated it as she dove, and a spray of blood spewed upwards as her gasp became a scream.

She had been drinking D's blood for over three years now, and had been his Familiar for the past two and a half. He drilled her over and over until she was sick and tired of it, and then the real training had begun. Quickly she mastered her panic and rolled to her feet.

She was soaked in blood which was now pouring from her neck. She pressed her hand to it and left it there in an attempt to staunch the flow before she could bleed out. Her knife was still in her hand, still sharper than it needed to be, and trembling only slightly in her grip.

Her attacker had taken a quick and staggering step backward and was clutching his shin with his off hand with blood between his fingers. The knife in his other hand was dripping and scarlet. She had no time to look at his dark features before he launched himself at her a second time.

She held her palm over her neck, not daring to feel how bad the wound was. Backpedaling, she raised her knife and let her body remember the martial arts drills D had run her through ad nauseum.

His knife flashed unpredictably in all directions. High on the left it glinted as he thrust at her temple and suddenly it rent across her stomach as she made to block. In frenzy he stabbed and slashed wildly.

No, not wildly. Each movement he made was punctuated by a burst of air from his nostrils. He was a trained fighter. Or trained killer. Tracy's own strikes and blocks were strong, all things considered. Thank God she drank D's blood when she had.

Nonetheless, even the small regenerative and augmentative properties it inferred on her would not be enough for the wounds she had received and was still taking. Nicks and cuts opened up along her arms, stomach, and legs. Not that her attacker was unscathed, but she was certainly bearing the brunt of the assault. Her own breathing was ragged and her vision was cloudy from the blood in her eyes and the blood leaving her body.

Post. Riposte. Attack. Defend.

Pain. Another blow connecting.

Post. Riposte. Attack. Slip.

More Pain.

She was slowing down, losing blood and losing time.

She blinked away the crimson tears welling in her eyes and immediately had to blink them away again. And again. And she knew what her only shot was.

She angled her body and took her hand away from her neck.

The cold gray eyes of her attacker were blinded by the deluge of arterial spray. His reaction lasted only half a second, but it was enough. Tracy slashed hard at his neck and buried her knife in his floating ribs.

And collapsed.

***

The man reeled backwards, one hand clutching his throat and the other pressed against his side. He jerked the knife out of his ribs and immediately wished that he hadn't. He staggered in a circle, glancing around the room for any sign of what he came for.

He quickened his pace and searched the hallway, opening doors and cupboards, clearing bookshelves. This was the right place; he knew it before even breaking into the garage. The girl with the knife only confirmed it further.

But he could not find his prize. Failure on any level would simply not be tolerated, and his job was only half done. His wounds were making him sloppy, and he was fully aware of this fact. He limped back the way he came, willing his pulse to slow and save what blood he had left. God knows he was going to need all the strength he could muster.

Half would have to do.

***

She woke up to her phone ringing.

Tracy opened one eye weakly and took a look around. The ring came again, a caribbean jingle that signaled Matt calling, followed by the chirp of a missed call. She traced the source of the sound to a spot on the floor to her right, about three feet away.

How am I alive? She thought to herself.

Continuing her visual sweep of the room, she brought her

gaze back to the foreground and gingerly brought her hand up to her neck.

It was the clay. She must have fallen onto her sculpture, and it was still wet enough to seal the wound somewhat. From there, the vampire blood in her system must have helped stitch her together. Or start to at least. She had lost so much blood, and definitely wasn't out of the woods yet.

She reached for the phone, which took several attempts and as many minutes. She pulled it back across the floor and looked at the screen to see six missed calls from Matt. Ordinarily she would be upset about his obsessive phone calls, but today it was a blessing. She also saw that the calls were at least fifteen minutes apart, which meant that she was out for a long time and in worse shape than she thought.

She opened the phone and called back.

***

Matt was almost to the lobby when Tracy finally called back.

"Hey babe, you go for a run or something?"

Only silence responded.

"Hello? Did you butt-dial me again? Hellooo?"

"Matt," came her voice finally and quietly. Too quietly.

"Tracy, what's wrong?"

Another pause. "I need you. Come quick."

"Babe?" He was getting very worried by now. He reached the elevator and hesitated before pushing the button to call it. An irritated woman behind him brusquely shouldered past and hit it herself.

"I'm hurt," Tracy finally said. "Really bad."

"Oh my God," Matt breathed, wheeling away from the elevator and breaking into a run back across the entryway. "Stay there and hold on, I'm calling 911 right now."

"NO!" Tracy said, a sudden strength working its way into the plea. "Just you, right now. Hurry," she trailed off, and said nothing else. Matt checked his phone. The line was still active, but

Tracy had stopped responding.

He called her name and shouted, but she said nothing back. He was about to hang up and call 911 anyway, but stopped short. She was an artist and prone to be eccentric about certain things, but hospitals and doctors were never one of them. Something in her voice was so certain, but Matt had to admit to himself that he had no idea what it was. He obeyed her wish and kept her line open.

He was in the car by then, pulling back out of the parking lot and tearing down the opposite lane of the highway. The traffic that choked him coming into work was still miraculously absent leaving it. Every few seconds he would tell her to hang on or give other encouragement. It wouldn't take him too long to get to her, but he knew that every second counted.

***

What seemed hours later, he ran inside the house. The scene that greeted him was a nightmare.

"TRACY!!" He screamed as he ran through the kitchen and into the living room.

She lay in a heap in the center of a Jackson Pollack painting done in all shades of red. The walls, the furniture, the ceiling were covered in crisscrossed patterns of blood. The floor was even worse. Matt slipped in several small puddles of the stuff as he ran to Tracy, who was herself resting in an even larger puddle around her clay and battered form.

His eyes stung as his mouth opened and closed wordlessly. He touched her face and took her hand.

"T-Tracy! I'm here! It's going to be ok!" He did not think it was going to be ok, and his voice did little to disguise it.

She opened her eyes and smiled.

"Babe," she whispered happily, deliriously. "Go downstairs and get D. Pull the Jameson."

"What? The old guy? Babe, you're not making sense. He's upstairs sleeping and the last thing you need is alcohol. No, I'm staying here with you and calling 911.”

"Matthew," was all she said. Her eyes, weak as they were, said the rest.

He ran to the basement door and threw it open. Flicking on a light, he jumped down the stairs.

"D?!" he called as he searched the space with his eyes. Under normal circumstances, he would have taken great pleasure in the basement. The ceiling was unexpectedly high, for one. There was a workout area in one corner with weights, machines, and a few punching bags. In another corner were three large bookshelves, a leather chair, and a table with a humidor box. Along one wall was a well-stocked bar.

Matt ran behind the bar and looked for the bottle of Jameson. What the hell was he was doing this for when Tracy was bleeding out slowly upstairs? He found it and yanked it hard, anxious to get back upstairs and finally call 911. Looking for an old man in a basement with alcohol was ridiculous. Enough with this nonsense, her life was at stake.

Except the bottle did not come down off the shelf. It tipped towards Matt and made a loud click, and a seam opened up in the wall next to the bar. Of all the things Matt expected, this was nowhere on the list.

"D??" he called, walking towards the crack in the wall and whatever lay beyond.

The wall suddenly swung wide open with a loud crash. Matt was heaved aside roughly and lightly, landing back behind the bar. A brief but intense rumble shook the basement stairs and once again light streamed down into the lower level.

Matt struggled to his feet and bounded toward the stairs, thoroughly disoriented. Back in the living room, a man was kneeling over Tracy and saying her name over and over. A man who was clearly not in his late seventies, but more along the lines of his late twenties or early thirties. Matt ran over to them.

"Who are you?" He demanded, moving to get between the man and Tracy.

"Help me get her clothes off," the other replied, pushing

Matt towards Tracy's feet and tearing her shirt open at the neck.

"Hey! What the fuck are you doing!?" Matt lunged for the man.

"I'M SAVING HER FUCKING LIFE AND YOU'RE HELPING ME." The reply came with such force that Matt literally froze in mid-lunge. Something in the combined elements of the man's eyes, voice, and posture made him instantly terrifying and absolute. Matt unbuttoned Tracy's pants.

Moving his glare back to Tracy's wounds, the man suddenly put his wrist in his mouth and tore a sizable wound into it. He stuffed his bloody wound into Tracy's mouth and performed the same action on his opposite wrist. Disgusted, Matt dove forward to stop him. His vision flashed as he was swatted away and sprawled on the ground. The man seated over his girlfriend hadn't even looked at him.

"I'm D," he said after a moment, wiping one bloody wrist on wound after wound. "You must be Mark."

"Matt."

"Right."

"Can I ask what the fuck you're doing smearing your blood on my girlfriend and pumping it into her mouth?"

"Fair question. It can't hurt at this point."

"The question?"

"No, the blood. She's lost a lot, and mine can heal her. At least she has both arms still, that's a real bitch to fix."

Matt was now completely lost and still too terrified of D to try and stop him. Nothing so far made any sense, and a strange smell was beginning to work its way into his nostrils. His eyes may have been playing tricks on him as well, but it looked like Tracy's wounds were smaller than they had been a moment ago. He pressed on, trying to get his bearings.

"You're not as old as she told me you were." He said.

"No, I'm probably older. By a lot."

To say that Matt had lost his patience would be a gross understatement. The entire day had been a surreal nightmare, his girlfriend was lying in blood and having more blood smeared onto her by the man she lived with who was not *Matt*. Trying to fight him was proving fruitless, and he hated feeling so helpless and ineffective. Additionally, the burnt meat and hair smell had now pervaded his senses and was driving him mad with irritation.

"Are you some kind of vampire or something?" He asked sarcastically.

"Bingo," said D without looking away from Tracy's wounds as they healed. "I know the curtains are drawn but could you pull the shades too? It's a bit toasty up here for me this early in the day."

***

Once Tracy had healed enough to move, they brought her down to the basement. Matt had said nothing since D told him he was a vampire and he reluctantly pulled down the window shades behind the curtains. The smell actually did abate to a large extent after that. He sat silently, intermittently staring into space and putting his head in his hands.

"Here." D's voice startled him out of another reverie. He held out a drink and Matt took it with shaking hands. He took a sip and gave the other a quizzical look.

"Mint julep," D replied knowingly to the unspoken question. "Too insecure to order it out at the bar, but still your favorite drink. Made with Wild Turkey, just like Mom and Dad used to make."

"How..." Matt began.

"I could make up some bullshit about vampires being mind readers, but Tracy told me. It'll help take the edge off."

"Tracy...is she gonna..."

"Be completely fine? Yes," D Finished. "She won't remember much of anything. My blood does that if you don't have much of your own left. Very handy, as you can imagine. I've seen worse. Much worse, in fact."

The ice clinked softly as Matt took another sip and turned it into a long draw. He shook his head. Tracy was bundled up in blankets and snuggled into D's coffin. A coffin! Matt found that it was surprisingly comfortable when he placed her inside, although it made for a disconcerting sight.

"I never knew about any of this," Matt said after the glass came down again. "I've been with Tracy for a year and a half now, the past year getting really serious. The whole time I thought she was a caretaker for an old guy that appreciated her art, and it turns out it's you. A weirdo claiming to be a vampire and putting a lot of effort into making it convincing."

"Such a gift for words."

"Sorry, not sorry."

"It's ok," D replied. "I know it looks weird and sketchy. I see it. I told her that it had to be that story, that the details about me would have to be hush-hush. I also told her to choose between taking care of me and being with you. She obviously really likes you, as she's done everything in her power to ignore that message and juggle both roles. What it is about you, I guess we'll see."

"Have you ever…" Matt raised his eyebrows.

"With *her*?" D grinned. "Never. Not even before you. It'd be like doing my sister. I'm a fucked up individual, but not *that* fucked up."

For the first time, Matt seemed to visibly relax. Tracy was going to be fine, she hadn't cheated on him, and the secrets she kept were for her own reasons. He still didn't believe this vampire story, but that could be addressed later. He finished his drink.

"It can't wait." D said suddenly.

"What can't?"

"You have to take this in. Now. It's a tough pill to swallow, I know. I see it in your face and body language. I'm not doing performance art here. I look like a regular person, but I'm not. I would be classified as a vampire. We are leaving in a while, and if you're not on board you're going to slow things down. Look at me."

D's irises changed both color and shape, drifting to a shade of gold with a narrow pupil. As he pulled back one black sleeve, his fingernails sprouted into bony claws. Opening his mouth, his canines began to extend as his skin seemed to pull taut against his skull. Slowly raking his hand down his arm, flesh parted and slowly stitched back together.

"*Believe.*" It was a command.

The voice echoed in his skull. He believed. Collapsing back into his chair in cold sweat, he watched as the other man's features shifted back. A silence fell.

"I need a favor or two from you, Matt." D prompted after a moment. "Tracy's taken a sick day today and the house is a mess. I need you to grab me her sculpting knife from upstairs. Feel free to clean too, if it'll help keep your mind occupied. I'd go up, but my soaps are on any minute now."

"You'd probably smell better down here," Matt admitted hazily. "Anything else?"

"Actually," D said thoughtfully. "Could you spare some blood?"

He paled. "I'll just go get that knife."

***

Matt bounded up the stairs, dizzy with fear as well with drink. Just when he thought things were going to be under control again and that he was safe, a vampire wanted to bite him and drink his blood. In every scary story, book, and movie he had experienced over the course of his life, that was never a good thing. He couldn't even handle getting blood drawn at the doctor's office, for God's sake.

He quickly found the knife on the floor of the living room, soaked and caked with blood like everything else in the vicinity. He picked it up and started back toward the basement, then stopped. Maybe he would clean up for a bit after all. The more time he spent upstairs was more time not having his neck bitten by a man who lived on a blood diet.

He had almost expended an entire bottle of Shout stain remover when D's voice floated up from the basement.

"Ohh Maaaaatt," he sang. "Did you find that knife? That's kind of the priority here."

"Just-just cleaning up quick!" He said hastily, squeezing the trigger on the cleaning bottle like his hand was in its death throes. The bottle was now firing blanks, and the room was still coated in blood.

"That can wait, thanks. Let's have that blade."

Matt sighed and trudged back to the basement stairs like he was walking the Green Mile and descended them with leaden feet. D was waiting at the bottom with his hand outstretched.

"Good." He said with a smile as he took the knife from Matt's hand. "How about that drink? I gave you one, it's only fair."

"I thought you were only being a good host!" Matt exclaimed, starting to panic and trying to edge his way sideways.

"Yes and no. Ordinarily I'd have Tracy help me out, but she's in no condition right now."

"So you *did* swap fluids!"

"Just the one. What do you say?"

"Isn't it kind of gay to bite a guy on the neck?" He was ashamed even as he said it but was beginning to panic now.

"Are you this insecure about everything? Fine, I'll bite you on the arm; you'll hardly feel anything anyways. I'll only take a little tiny bit, less than I usually take even from Tracy."

Matt was out of responses and up against the back of a leather chair. D hadn't moved. Reluctantly, he rolled up his sleeve.

"Just…please don't hurt me. I mean…be careful."

"It's your first time, I'll be gentle." D winked and moved forward.

Matt reclined the chair and turned his face away, eyes shut tightly. He felt a light prick in the middle of his arm, like someone had poked him with a pair of needles. He started to feel lightheaded, and he willed himself to keep it together.

Then, surprisingly, he felt great; in fact, he felt deliriously great. He opened his eyes and found his vision rippling gently and his light-headedness resolving into gentle disorientation. D was seated in the other leather chair next to him.

"Mmm, minty!" D exclaimed with a sigh. "My blood's probably kicking in now, so you sit back and relax."

Matt did just that.

***

D shifted his eyes from one prone human form in the basement to the other and sighed. He was not prepared for this, not by a long shot. He was exhausted and had used most of his blood to make sure Tracy would actually live. He drank more from Matt than he had intended or conveyed, but not enough to really weaken him or bring about the usual amnesia. All three occupants of the house were currently anemic. A pleasant thought, he reflected sarcastically.

His attention turned on the knife, dripping onto the mahogany table in front of him. D picked it up and turned it over in his hand, eyeing the blood patterns on the blade carefully. This was one of the few things in the house that did not have Tracy's blood on it, but rather that of her attacker. The man who had broken into his home and taken nothing, only assailing his Familiar with lethal intent. It did not bode well at all.

D put the knife up to his mouth and ran his tongue along the sides of the blade, licking as much blood off as he could. He closed his eyes as he swallowed it and seemed to focus on the impressions he received from it.

A casual observer would have seen his brows furrow in concentration and then flare upwards in surprise, driven by a rippling spasm that rocked his features and fired a shudder through the rest of his body.

D felt the fear and dogged determination of the man, saw shadowy hands press on his shoulders, and heard screams. One after the other, the screams started quietly and rose in a cacophony. The shadow hands detached themselves from the man's shoulders. D followed them back to their origin, a monolithic entity of darkness, which in turn seemed to shift and focus on D. A final scream ended the Impression, one all too familiar to him.

"Fuck!" he exclaimed with a start, rocking forward with eyes wide. He threw the knife and reached for his cigarette case.

The knife stuck squarely in the spine of one of the books on the bookshelf across from him.

He clicked the case closed, lit the cigarette, and took a long drag. He blew a smoke ring and blew the rest out through his nostrils. He took another drag and reached for his phone. Blowing out the smoke in an exasperated manner, he dialed her from his contact list. As expected, she answered after barely the first ring.

"D. How nice of you to call after only eighty years."

"Rebecca, it's good to hear your voice. Only seventy-eight years by my count, give or take six months."

There was a short huff on the line that may have been either amusement or scorn.

"I never heard back from you. No one did. We knew you were still alive, but wanted to give you some space before reaching out."

D took another drag on his cigarette before answering.

"Well, someone just reached out really hard. They broke in and tried to kill my Familiar today."

"Oh my god are-"

"No, it's ok, we're all fine now. After patching up the kid I assessed the damage. I got a vague Impression and I think a family trip is in order."

Rebecca paused before asking her next question.

"Who else have you called?"

"Ouch, really?" D feigned hurt. "You're my first. As ever." He added. "I hate to impose, but I don't trust anyone more. Any chance there would be room for three at the ranch?"

"Three?"

"My Familiar's familiar. Just like to put myself higher on the totem pole when possible. I get a feeling he might be along for the ride."

"I'll have the rooms ready for you, and I can send a cab in a few minutes."

"Rebecca, really. Thank you."

There was the briefest of pauses on the other line.

"It'll be good to see you, D. Be safe."

***

Rebecca put down the phone and shook her head, running her fingers through her dark brown hair. She pulled out her master schedule from her desk drawer and flipped it open.

He wouldn't have called if he didn't want them trained. D had a myriad of other houses and safe-houses he could have gone to in order to weather any particular difficulty. He might have missed her company, but Rebecca wouldn't flatter herself by allowing the thought to cross her mind. Eighty years was a long time for anyone, though in his case it was certainly understandable.

Pulling herself from her reverie, she examined the schedule for the next month's classes. There were exactly zero open slots.

"Inconvenient as always," she muttered to herself. Either she would have to squeeze them into full class-loads or she would have to teach them herself. D could probably teach them, but something in his voice told her his stay would be somewhat shorter.

Thankfully, most of the clients staying at the Ranch slept in the main community bunk, or with their Sires if they happened to be staying as well. Two rooms remained free; Rebecca was certain that D's group could work out sleeping arrangements.

She decided she would teach them herself. Her assistants could run the other classes; they had certainly had enough experience by now. This way she could try to get a read on D while he was here, for all the good it would do her.

"Will," she said, punching the intercom button.

"Yes, Ms. Walker?" came the reply.

"I need you and Joe to get the van and do a transport."

"Of course. For what time this evening?"

"Right now. I'll text you the address."

"Certainly, Ms. Walker. Anything else?"

"No. Call if you have any trouble, I'm going back to bed. See you tonight."

***

A few hours later, a large white moving van backed into the driveway of D's home. Matt watched through the curtains as asked, coffee in hand. He had woken to D shaking his shoulder, remembering only bringing the knife downstairs as asked. D had assured him he was fine and asked him if he could move both Matt's car and the one in the garage out to the street.

He went to the basement door and called down to D that the truck had arrived.

"The movers or the cleaners?" came D's response.

"Big truck; has to be movers."

"Super." Another dry response.

There was a knock on the front door and Matt went to answer. Two men stood at the entrance in plain shirts and jeans and introduced themselves as Will and Joe.

"Are you the Familiar here?" Will asked.

"What?" Matt gave a quizzical look. "No, I don't live here. My girlfriend does, with D." He still didn't like the sound of that. "They're both downstairs," he added.

The two men nodded.

"Is the garage free?" the one named Joe asked.

"Yeah, the cars are out on the street there," Matt pointed.

"Great, thanks" Will said, moving past Matt and into the house while Joe went back to the truck. "If you could gather your things, we can be on our way in a few minutes."

Matt went back down to the basement to relay the news. D nodded and pointed to a couple duffel bags packed by the stairs

"Bags or broad?" he asked.

Matt gave another of his uncomprehending looks that were quickly becoming his new trademark.

"Gear or girl?" D said again, jerking his thumb back to the coffin where Tracy was still sleeping.

"Oh, Tracy!" Matt exclaimed, moving toward her. "You could show a little more respect considering she almost died protecting you today."

"Fine. Sorry," D grunted as he layered himself in clothing to protect every inch from the sun. "I'm a little bitchy when I'm tired and hungry. And up all day." Looking like a cross between a ninja and an Inuit, he grabbed the duffel bags and plodded up the stairs.

Matt bent over Tracy and kissed her cheek.

"We have to go now, sweetie," he said softly, wrapping his hands around her waist and legs.

"Mmm," she hummed weakly and put her head against his chest. She felt lighter than he expected her to, and he wasn't sure if that was a good or bad sign.

Carefully, he made his way upstairs with her. The van had backed halfway into the garage and effectively sealed off all light. The door was closed to the top of the back, and thick black sheets hung from either side. The doors to the back of the truck were open, revealing a surprisingly furnished and comfortable looking room inside. D was already seated on one of the three couches and checking one of the two mini-fridges next to it.

Matt laid Tracy down on one of the couches and sat on the third. A flat screen television adorned one wall of the room, and a remote was affixed to the central coffee table with Velcro.

"This is amazing," Matt whispered in awe.

"It certainly is," D agreed from beneath his sunglasses and scarf, obviously ready for the movers to close the doors so he could pull them off. He flicked a switch and the two floor length lamps turned on, as well as a recessed neon light that traced the outline of the cab along the floor.

"All set, folks?" one of the movers asked as he popped his head through the back door. When he received the affirmative, he gave a thumbs-up and closed the door with a heavy thud. Closely following this was the reverberating clang of the heavy latch being locked down. D nodded at Matt as they felt the moving truck pull away from his former home and begin its journey onwards.

****

Miles away, a sleek black van pulled into a desolate gravel parking lot that wrapped around an abandoned and forgotten industrial complex. Faded signs and broken windows looked out forlornly from the crumbling walls. The air was tainted with the emptiness that the place evoked.

How many miles it had been, the man was not sure. He had been unconscious for some time during the ride, in fact. He lay panting across the seat of the van as one of the men continued to dress his wounds. He had cuts up and down his body, on his arms, legs, and torso. His worst wounds were his neck and his side, where the woman had slashed and stabbed him.

The woman. His head lolled back at the painful memory. Outmaneuvered and overcome by a woman. He had done so much better in so many worse situations; how was he going to explain this to the one who had sent him? He had been collected precisely because of his reputation as a fearless and ruthless killer.

The van pulled into a small garage tucked into the side of the building. The driver parked and walked around to open the sliding door and let his passenger out.

"Out you go, Red," he said as the man slowly clambered down from the vehicle. He had driven the man called Red a few times before with no incidents. This time, however, he looked like hell. Bandages were hastily applied to his neck and side, but a myriad of smaller cuts continued to bleed slowly. He moved with a slowness that belied his pain. The two made eye contact briefly as Red pulled his jacket around himself a little tighter.

"Good luck," the driver said to him. Red gave a nod of assent and limped off into the shadows.

He had never been to this building before, he knew that for certain. He had spoken with his employer in person only once, and after that he had only received brief phone calls or emails. The calls and emails were always untraceable, and his first visit was also marked by a blindfolded van ride.

A sense of déjà vu overtook Red as he made his way through the darkened corridors. The entire complex appeared to be empty and vacant, but something about the quiet thrum beneath his feet hinted that there was more there than met the eye. He had no idea which way he was supposed to travel through the labyrinthine halls, and yet his feet moved with purpose along an unseen path. It was almost as if he was being pulled inexorably along, and it was an unsettling feeling.

Along the dim corridors he walked, his footfalls echoing off the mute gray walls, until he came to the door. It was a standard double-wide door, and the last thing in his path. Red took a deep breath, pushed it open, and walked through.

The darkness inside was palpable, and became complete when the doors quietly locked behind him. He didn't dare make a move, only waited to be greeted. The sense of déjà vu reached a crescendo, and the silent darkness enveloped him. It must have only a few moments, but it felt like eternity there in the blackness.

"So," a voice finally ventured after all that time. "Here you are at last."

It chilled Red to the bone. The voice was immediately behind him, and he could feel the breath behind the words. He was close enough to the door that no one should have been able to sneak up that close undetected. The voice was definitely masculine, but high and almost melodic. The soft resonance and dim echo given off by it let Red know that the room he stood in was much larger than he initially thought.

"I came as quick as I could, given the situation," Red stated, eyes darting. His eyes did not seem to be adjusting to the darkness at all. If anything, the room seemed blacker than it had when he entered.

There was a rustle of fabric across the room in front of him, and the voice spoke up again from a new location.

"The situation," it said mockingly. "Where you were unable to fulfill your end of our contract. Was it the master of the house that gave you those scratches?" It was the same voice, to be sure, but to Red it sounded deeper and somehow more gravelly. He had no idea how his employer already knew about his failure, but it would be useless to sugarcoat anything at this point.

"No, it was a woman who did it. She was faster and stronger than any man I've ever fought, but it's no excuse. I have her blood, though." He held up a sealed plastic bag containing the knife he had used with her.

Instantly the package was torn from his hands as if sucked away by a tornado. In another far corner of the room came the sound of the bag's seal being broken and the knife clicking open. Red wondered again just how many people were in the group representing his employer.

"I see," came the voice again, this time by his opposite shoulder. "She outmatched you, and no wonder. How many other items were you able to maintain?"

Red was somewhat taken aback at the blatant insult. He had never been outmatched. Even in that Russian prison operation, he had once killed two huge men armed with buck-knives while he himself was weaponless. However, he sensed it would be stupid to argue now.

"Nothing else," he admitted. "I was too injured to make it far into the house. I had to leave with what I could."

"That's a shame," the voice replied from next to him. "Tell me, how many contracts have you done for me?"

"Three."

"And how many people per contract?"

"At least two."

"And how many special items did I ask for?"

"At least one per contract."

"I've paid you a small fortune, erased your debts, and bought you a house. And now you stop performing your duties. I selected you because I thought you were the perfect man for the job, but now I see that it's gotten to be a bit too much for you. You're using *half* of your talents and getting *half* of the work done."

While the voice remained the same in volume, it increased steadily in intensity. Despite being nearly backed up to the door, Red felt a hand on his back, sliding slowly down his spine. His discomfort was reaching a peak, and he forced himself not to sprint away blindly.

"Maybe you're only *half* the man I needed after all."

The hand stopped at the small of his back and began to squeeze slowly. Red wasn't sure, but he almost thought he felt pointed claws. As the fingers curled in more, he was certain that they were indeed claws and could contain his fear no longer. He cried out and lurched forward, but the grip on his spine was simply too strong. Dauntless, the clawed hand crushed tighter and tighter. Fingers pierced his skin and dug through muscle fibers, clutching at his backbone directly and continuing their march.

There were few people on the planet that could withstand that much pain, and Red was not among them. He cried and shrieked in agony, writhing and struggling. Finally, the cloaked figure behind him closed his fist, crumpling his spine like an empty can. Shock immediately took Red's consciousness, and all faded to darkness.

The hand dropped his limp body to the floor. With what migt have been a dismissive wave, two attendants manifested from the shadows and the body was dragged from the room. They returned to the eyes in the dark, grim and determined.

There was work to do.

***

Matt put down his magazine and looked at D as he reclined at the end of the mobile room. Only the occasional bump and quiet rumble of the engine reminded him that they were in fact in the back of a truck instead of a living room. D lay very still, propped up to see the television and still clad in several layers of clothing while sporting sunglasses.

"You gonna change out outfits anytime soon?" Matt asked.

"You trying to catch a peek?" came the reply. After a pause, he added "Nope. Shit happens. Traffic accidents, storms, all that. Take no chances outside the home, remember that."

He said all of this without moving or otherwise acknowledging Matt. His delivery was always deadpan, but Matt noticed that over the course of the ride he had increasingly lacked any intonation at all. Matt suspected he was more tired and upset than he let on. Several times he wondered if the man was asleep or worse; only the mysteriously changing channels suggested otherwise.

"What's going on, D? And where are we going? I know this is worse than it seems, and it seems pretty bad. You had a break-in and Tracy was attacked with a knife in your house. She seems fine now, thank God, but I'm really not used to this cloak and dagger stuff. I disappeared from work, and that's probably the end of that."

"You hated that place anyway," D replied. "You have more skill than they know or admit to, and you were essentially being paid to be drained for their benefit." He smiled. "I guess I can offer you the same job, essentially. I'll just utilize your talents a bit more, drain you a bit less often, and take more blood when I do. I'll also pay better. You did pretty well for the first bite; I lied and took a bit more than I said I would."

"You...you bit me?" Matt asked. "How did you know about my work? Did Tracy say something?"

"You've always lied to her about liking it," D said, finally moving to stand up and stretch. "And yes I bit you. You probably won't remember; that's just the way it works. At least the first few times. The more you get used to my blood, the more you'll be able to tolerate it."

He moved to the two small refrigerators and opened one. Seeing the assortment of beer and soft drinks, he closed it and opened the second one. Inside was a single carafe and one large mug. He took these out and poured a thick dark stream into the mug.

"A warmer for the blood," He smiled at Matt's obvious discomfort and took a sip. "Ooh, Jenny's still there! Hints of spice." He tilted his head back and savored the taste. "About the work thing, I knew all that once I tasted your blood. It's a little talent of my own. Not common, but not too rare either. Your blood says a lot about you. A *lot*." He left it at that and sat back down.

"As for where exactly we're headed, I have no idea. She has a couple operations and moves around a bit for safety. But it'll be a safe-house owned by a friend where we can get back on our feet and figure out what to do next. More of a safe-*camp*, now that I think of it. You'll see. You might even like it."

Matt got up and grabbed a beer for himself. He was numb. He had been bitten? And his blood apparently told D about himself. Talking with D still felt like an awkward exchange between a current and an ex-boyfriend of the same girl. What was most troubling is that Matt wasn't sure which man was which.

He sat down next to Tracy and touched her cheek as D changed the channel again from news to soap operas. Her skin was warm but not hot, and her coloring had returned. D had assured him that she needed rest more than anything now, and so Matt kept her bundled up comfortably on the longest couch in the room.

Not the longest couch in the room. In the back of truck. A truck, for God's sake.

What had he gotten himself into?

***

They arrived after dark. An intercom buzzed in the compartment and the drivers let them know they were entering the "delivery area". Departure was a short wait away, and Matt was certainly thankful. He stood and stretched.

"So you really have no idea where we are." Matt stated.

"Nope. Could be in part of a casino or hotel, college campus, maybe even a hole in the ground. Wherever it's set up, it'll be run the same. No schools like hers out there, that's for sure."

"School?"

"Nickname. My friend runs a facility that trains and educates Familiars."

"Why go through all of that?" Matt asked.

"Think about it," D replied. "You can go it alone as a vampire, sure. But there's risk. Weakness during daylight hours is obvious, same goes for reliable food supply. Solitude saves money but creates other problems."

"What about hiring bodyguards?" Matt countered. "And blood banks? I know there have to be other ways of getting blood than from biting people."

"Yes and no. There are ways to scrape by, but they suck. In a bind, you can make do with what you have, just like the dollar menu or the back of the fridge when your standards get low enough. It's just not as good, and not as good for you. Having just one or two people to help out consistently helps you keep a low profile and avoid drawing attention from the rest of the world. What did you think about me before you met me?"

Matt shrugged.

"I knew almost nothing. You were just an older man that needed some extra help and could afford a live-in caregiver."

"And what do you think of me now?"

Matt paused. So much had happened in so little time that he really had not processed one bit of it emotionally. His girlfriend had lied about her job, lied about this man in particular and what her duties were to him. He wasn't really *human*, in the main sense of the word, and that would probably take an even longer time to strike him. He had left work before a very important meeting and was more than likely unemployed now. On top of it all, he was being taken to an unknown location in the back of a moving vehicle. The man across from him lived with his girlfriend and claimed to drink blood for a living. Matt opened his mouth to answer D's question, then shook his head and closed it again.

"My point exactly," D nodded knowingly. "Educate and familiarize a few trustworthy people and we won't have to make as many people so upset."

The room seemed to slant suddenly and they knew that the truck was pulling into an underground parking area. They slowed to a halt and the engine powered off. The rumbling and thrumming had become constant traveling companions with them, and it was somewhat jarring to lose them both at once.

The back doors swung open as the drivers from the

cab ushered them out. Matt and D stepped out into a large underground garage and parking structure. D smiled and stretched his arms. Matt scowled and looked around.

The building had higher ceilings than he would have thought and was very well lit with large, pale fluorescent lights. His adrenaline shock was wearing off at last from that morning and the numbness concerning the astronomical improbability of his situation – the goddamn *strangeness* – was breaking. He had been kidnapped and shuttled halfway around the state, maybe the country. He was in no mood for more.

Then he saw her.

"D!" echoed a bright voice from across the cavernous space. Through the thin crowds of people loading boxes onto and from various trucks stepped one of the most striking women Matt had ever seen. He was terrible at guessing ages, but she couldn't have been older than her late twenties. Her auburn hair hung in loose curls and bounced lightly as she strode towards them. More impressive than her physical beauty was the way she carried herself. She took long, graceful strides and had an air of gentle command uncommon for one so young.

She smiled and gave D a short embrace. D pointed Matt out and she shook his hand warmly.

"Rebecca," She said.

"Hi. I'm…mm…mm." Matt finished.

She had already turned and leapt into the van.

"Will! Chair!" she called.

She hopped back down as one of the drivers brought over a wheelchair. She nodded at Matt, and an embarrassing moment later he realized she was asking him to bring Tracy out of the van and hopped back in.

As he hefted her body into his arms, Matt realized again how light she seemed and frowned worriedly. As soon as he placed Tracy in the chair, she was whisked away by the man called Will before he could open his mouth to protest.

"Forget it, she'll be fine," D called over from a hushed conversation with Rebecca. "Come on, let's get settled in."

Matt matched pace with the two as they walked down another hallway away from the large loading area. The concrete walls gave way to plush walls and velvet curtains.

"Where exactly are we?" Matt finally managed to ask, not quite making eye contact with Rebecca.

"After what D's told me so far, I don't think now is the best time to tell you everything," She told him consolingly. "But for starters, we happen to be in a secluded resort and spa. It's highly exclusive and in the middle of the slow season, so you'll be safe here for as long as you need to stay. You'll be in the private side of the building, only other initiates."

"Other initiates?"

"That's right," She nodded knowingly. "You've had a very long day and probably have a lot to digest. Let me show you your room. D, I'll meet up with you in the bar."

D nodded his approval and stepped to a nearby elevator. Rebecca took Matt by the arm and he felt his ears go red.

"Shall we?"

***

The room was breathtaking.

It was actually unfair to call it a room; Matt's quarters were more lavish than the average honeymoon suite. Luxurious chairs and a loveseat circled a wide fireplace, over which hung a large flatscreen television. The full bar had seen sat against the other wall. In the corner, a hot tub bubbled gently. It looked as if the suite took up a large portion of one of the hotel floors.

"Initiate sector," Rebecca smiled. "I know it must be hard to get pulled into it without warning, but this life does have its benefits." She handed him a slim black card that was heavier than it looked, and had no markings whatsoever. "Your key, your credit card, and basically your badge. Show it wherever you go around here and we'll take care of you."

Matt turned it over in his hand. "How can I afford-" he began, but Rebecca smiled and shook her head, auburn curls bouncing.

"It won't cost you a dime. You've done a lot today,

and unfortunately it looks like you'll have a lot more to look forward to. Enjoy this one upgrade on me." Her smile widened mischievously. "The rest is up to you, on D's tab."

Matt couldn't help but smile at that. For the first time since that morning, he felt some measure of peace. He opened his mouth to ask one last question, but Rebecca held up a hand.

"Tracy's going to be fine," she assured him. "She'll be back with you in a day or two, maybe even tomorrow." She took him by the shoulders and looked into his eyes while he did his best to keep the heat from rising in his cheeks. She was even more stunning up close.

"You've been though a lot today; seen a lot, done a lot, traveled a lot, and *lost* a lot. I know you have more questions and worries. We'll take care of everything, starting tomorrow morning. Tonight, your job is to rest so you can have the energy to deal with it. Take a bath, make a drink, watch TV, and get some room service. I'm sure you haven't eaten, and they tell me the duck is amazing. We'll get through every question and settle every concern. The trick is to think of it like eating an elephant."

Matt cocked an eyebrow. "And how is that?"

She smiled and replied, "One bite at a time."

Matt smiled back, but couldn't help noticing that her canines were quite pointed.

***

D sat at the hotel bar alone, hand on his chin, and feeling troubled. So much had happened and so fast that he truthfully had processed little more than Matt had. His home had been broken into, his familiar and confidante had been brutally assaulted and escaped with her life only barely.

But why?

Instinctually, he knew that was just the first wave, the falling rock that signaled a landslide. And so, barely an hour after the incident he had packed and left his home of fifty years and fled like a refugee. Not to mention fleeing with an uninitiated and decidedly idiotic human whose disappearance would not go unnoticed for very long. It was all just one throbbing pain in the ass.

He needed a drink.

As if on cue, the bartender sidled over. A well-dressed young man, he placed a napkin in front of D and smiled.

"What can I get for you, sir?" he asked.

"'Jenny around?" D replied "I got her sample flight earlier."

The bartender nodded politely and disappeared into the back. A moment later a busty blonde woman emerged and clapped her hands together with a smile.

"D! Get over here you! I hoped Becky would send mine on the van. I've missed you!" She came around the bar, kissed him on the cheek, and sat next to him.

"Jenny, Jenny, a sight for sore eyes," D smiled back. He lifted her had to kiss it, then turned it over and winked. "May I?"

"Of course!" She giggled. He bent low and gingerly bit in. She winced slightly as his teeth broke through the soft flesh of her wrist and punctured the veins below, but never lost her smile. She sighed and closed her eyes patiently. "You're sweet, that's why I like you. Thanks for going easy on me."

D lifted his head and wiped his mouth. Taking a napkin, he pressed it against her wrist.

"Don't know what you mean," he winked. "You're the best; I'm just treating you accordingly." Sensing movement from the doorway behind him, he closed his hands over hers. "I've got some business to go over with Rebecca now, but maybe we can catch up later."

Jenny smiled and nodded knowingly and took her leave. Rebecca walked over and filled the empty seat.

"Always the ladies man," she teased. "Feeling better? You can't have had much to drink today. Not to pry, but that seemed like a small sip compared with what most of the guests drink, even casually."

"I have enough sins to keep me busy without adding gluttony to the list." He replied. "And I know she's in demand here. All those teeth are bound to make someone sensitive, even if they don't leave a mark."

He paused a moment and simply looked at Rebecca. The sight of her was refreshing and painful all at once. She seemed to reciprocate the sentiment.

"So," He said simply.

"So," She agreed. She waved the bartender back over. "Two please. Special for me, whiskey on the rocks with two splashes for my guest here."

The bartender nodded and went to work. As he set about to make a complicated-looking martini for Rebecca, she turned to D.

"We'll need these," she said. "First off, the council is going to want to see you. I know," she added, noting the surprised and indignant twist his face had taken. "It can't be helped. It's been a long time and they've been respectful. That part will just be a formality."

The bartender placed the finished martini in front of her, a crimson concoction which smelled light and fruity and only slightly coppery.

"That part?" D asked, knowing he would regret it.

"You're not the only one who's been attacked recently," She said finally, sipping her drink and nodding to the bartender. "You are, however, the only one to have survived."

The bartender finished pouring D's whiskey, pulled out a warm carafe of blood and added two generous splashes to it. Sensing the tension in their conversation, he produced a small sewing needle from under his watch and pricked a finger.

"For your trouble, sir," He said as he squeezed several drops of blood into the glass before vanishing into the back again.

D took one sip and then another as the news sank in.

"Who?" He asked finally.

"Three so far. Mira, Klaus, and Stephan."

D took a large sip of his drink and closed his eyes. The pain and nausea from swallowing the whiskey raw rather than through a bloodstream burned him, and he held onto the sensation. A long moment of silence passed.

"Shit. I guess I'll be going then. When do they want to see me?"

"They have transportation coming now," she sighed.

"I hate that place," he admitted as he looked at her.

"As well you should," she said as she met his gaze.

D sighed and took another drink. Things were moving again, and too fast. Not even a day ago he was living comfortably and relatively quietly. Now he was hiding out and avoiding getting murdered, apparently.

"At least I'm not Matt," he thought out loud as he drained his glass.

"Oh good, you're still awful after all," Rebecca shook her head and smiled. "What do you want to do with him?"

"You don't have any pupils you can spare, do you?"

She shook her head.

He sighed and tapped his empty glass against his forehead. He really didn't want to say this.

"We might as well enroll him. They know Tracy's face now, not to mention whatever they could get from her blood if they have a Sommelier. The kid's nowhere near ready, but if we push him through the crash course at a high enough pace he might just be able to scrape by. Can you do it?"

"I'll pitch in myself," she replied immediately. "I'm bored with business administration; it'll be good to get some hands-on exercise again. You might want to go let him know before you leave, though. I'd hate to be in his shoes tomorrow otherwise."

***

Matt cracked open the cocktail shaker and poured himself a drink. He raised the glass to his lips for the first sip, grimaced, and began to pour it out into the sink. It was his third attempt, and he couldn't make a drink to save his life. He hadn't been able to even since his college days, really. He checked himself as he realized that the liquor he was pouring out was top shelf quality, then remembered that the bill was D's and overturned the glass completely.

Searching through the room's bar he found a bottle of red wine and gave himself a generous portion. He made his way back to the hot tub, his attention split between the gentle allure of the crackling fireplace, the high-definition movie, and the excellent meal on the tray before him. The duck was just as exquisite and aromatic as Rebecca made it out to be, and the succulent orange glaze made it unlike anything he had been served before.

A knock at the door brought his head up with a jerk. Grabbing a towel, he clambered from the tub and made his way to the entrance. As he cracked the door, D pushed his way into the room, knocking Matt onto his back.

"Of all times for you to be naked," he muttered as he bent to pull the young man to his feet.

"What the hell was that about!?" Matt shouted. "I finally catch a break, eat some real food and try to escape from the shitstorm you made and you barge in here and knock me on my ass!"

Clearly that was the last straw for Matt, who had been trying so hard to hold it together all day. His voice was strained and breaking, and circles were beginning to darken under his eyes. Seeing this, D felt a measure of pity and regret for both what the boy had gone through and what was apparently in store.

"I'm an ass, I know, I get it," he began. "Sorry. That's just a taste of what's coming for you, so make sure you're more careful with her tomorrow morning."

Matt gave D the uncomprehending look that quickly and unfortunately becoming his trademark.

"Look," D went on, "I've gotta take a trip in a little bit. I won't be gone long, but I have some things to take care of. You can leave tomorrow if you want to, but Tracy has to stay here, even after she gets better. Whoever wants her dead probably knows everything about her already, including whatever she knows about you. If you decide to leave tomorrow, you'll essentially be going wit-pro. New life, new job, new name. We can do our best to keep you safe that way, we have the resources."

"Why would I want to do that?" Matt said. "I'm not just gonna abandon Tracy and start some new fake life. Who the hell are you people anyway? How could you afford that?"

"Matt, there aren't many other people like me," D said after a pause. "Vampire people. But we've been around a long time. Long enough to make connections where needed and enough money for comfort and privacy. If you choose to stay here, it won't just be out of the goodness of my heart. The only way I can swing it is if you learn to be like Tracy."

"What is she to you anyway?"

"The word we use is 'Familiar'. Even though plenty of vampire myths are complete bullshit, it's true that I'm mostly useless during the day. A vampire's familiar keeps watch over them by day, ensuring privacy and protecting them from possible harm. Tracy lived in the house with me like a live-in home health aide, keeping up my cover. She was also there to protect me when that intruder broke in, and many familiars have found themselves in similar situations over the years. Sometimes it's mundane crime, plain and simple. Most times, though, it's not. If you stay you'll learn more, but high vampire society and politics are… complicated."

"Complicated."

"Don't give me that tone. Anyway, I can't force you to do anything, like I said before. You can take the blue pill and leave, but you'll have to say goodbye to Tracy first. If she's awake yet."

That was the sobering thought that gave him pause. Matt's life was none too exciting (not counting recent developments) and Tracy was easily the brightest part of it. His job was unfulfilling and time consuming, but it had allowed him to slowly save up for a ring. Not just a sliver of diamond in a wiry gold band; a real, dazzling, impressive piece of art that he wanted to put on the hand of the most beautiful artist to illuminate and color his life.

The money he had saved up for that ring was set aside in a special savings account, hidden away as it were. If he were to take this deal, to disappear safely and even comfortably, there would be no ring. There would be no Tracy. As much as his emotions about her at present were in turmoil, he was sure at least that he did not want to end here and now with her.

"I'll stay."

Two words, barely whispered, broke his silence as his eyes

returned back to D's. He felt his feet brush the ground again, no longer lost in the daze that the unreality of his life had cast on him. He was sure about that one thing, and that certainty gave him the strength he needed.

"Good," D smiled, clapping him on the shoulder. "Get some rest tonight, and secure all the locks on the door. When you answer it in the morning, step as far back as you can."

"What?" Matt asked, likely for the thousandth time.

D gave him an appraising look and shook his head with a sly grin.

"Never mind, you'll be fine. Probably."

***

The morning broke gently over Matt and his eyes fluttered slowly open. In actuality, he could not be sure that it was truly morning. The hallways leading to his room had no windows, and even his suite's walls lacked a single pane. There were plenty of lamps and even a large piece of backlit glass artwork, but he would have needed a clock to tell him the time of day. Speaking of which, there were no clocks anywhere, not even in the television displays. He couldn't even find his phone.

The door knocked for a second time and Matt realized that was what was waking him up. He sat up in his king size bed, throwing down the Egyptian cotton sheets, and looked around blearily as he made his way toward the door. The fire had burned low while he slept, the gentle crackle the only noise in the room. The television had turned off automatically, he supposed. Whatever traffic came through the area obviously couldn't make enough noise to filter up this high in the building. It was one of the more peaceful awakenings he had had.

"Who is it?" He called out hoarsely, seemingly trying his voice on for the first time.

"Breakfast," a pleasant female voice answered.

"Hold on," Matt checked himself for pants as he ambled to the doorway. Finding himself appropriate, he leaned on the doorframe as he unlocked and turned the latch.

Immediately the calm of his morning exploded as if he had

stepped on a landmine. The door ruptured inward on its hinges as the friendly-sounding lady crashed her way into the room, knocking the door into Matt's head and Matt's head into the floor. Immediately he felt knees pressing on his ribs with the force of bodyweight behind them. He raised his arms to move them away, but his wrists were snatched out of the air and wrenched into awkward and painful positions. He heard a metallic click and realized his hands were being cuffed in that odd position, one elbow above his head and one behind his back.

Matt barely registered any of this, his senses reeling. The door had sent white flashes into his eyes on contact with his skull, and before he had even hit the ground the air was full of the sound of screaming. Angry, accusing screams, delivered directly to his ears by his assailant from a full four inches away.

"WHERE IS HE GET ON THE FLOOR WHERE THE FUCK IS HE DON'T EVEN THINK ABOUT IT YOU PIECE OF SHIT I'LL GIVE YOU SOMETHING TO THINK ABOUT"

Matt instinctively tried to kick out with his legs, either to get into a better position or to kick at his attacker. However, she was seated comfortably on his midsection and he was pinned hopelessly. From this angle he could see that she was in her late 30's and Hispanic with a short and muscular build. Her black hair was pulled back into a tight ponytail and her bright eyes shone with malice.

As she clicked the handcuffs shut she stopped screaming at him long enough to sit up straight. As she did so, she removed a pistol from a shoulder holster and cocked it. She grabbed his jaw and pulled downward, forcing the gun into his mouth with the other hand. Matt felt the cold steel slide over his tongue and gagged, his teeth rattling uncomfortably against the barrel.

"I'm gonna take this out in 2 seconds and you're gonna tell me the only thing I need to hear, or it's going back in and the cleaning lady's gonna need overtime to get your brains out of everything. Understand?" She half-whispered, half-growled the threat, and Matt distinctly wished that she had simply kept screaming.

Before he could think about what to say, the gun barrel came scraping out of his mouth. He looked at her in terror, unblinking and silent with his mouth hanging desperately open. One wrong word would be the end. Where? Who? What? None of those seemed like reasonable replies. He realized he was about to wet himself, and with all his might he willed himself to at least hold that together. A single tear escaped down each cheek. His mouth was still open.

"Enough, Rita," came another female voice. A familiar one.

Rebecca walked into the room and cast a piteous smile down at him and apologetically shook her head.

"How'd he do?" She asked.

The woman on his stomach grunted. "Just like I thought. Cried like a bitch." She shifted off of him and stood up, grabbing one of his ankles and pulling it to the side. "No piss though, so a little better I guess. I once made a cop shit himself." She said the last to Matt with a smirk.

Matt's humiliation and fear were quickly metabolizing themselves into anger and indignation. In the last 48 hours his life was turned upside down, his girlfriend was brutally assaulted, he was practically kidnapped by people who claimed to be vampires, and here he was being assaulted himself by these same people. Where did they get off? He couldn't contain himself any longer and the last part broke free through his mouth.

"Where do you people get off!?" He shouted hoarsely "Do you have any idea what I've been through? Do you do this for fun? Kidnap people and bring them to your clubhouse so you can beat the crap out of them and scare them so you can pretend to be vampires? This is bullshit! Completely stupid and insane! Vampires don't exist, you're just sick rich bastards with a weird fetish! I want out!" The hazy memory of D commanding Matt to *believe* was no longer enough.

Suddenly Rebecca was on top of him and pressing him against the floor. She opened her mouth and bared her teeth, a strange hissing noise emitting from her throat. In horror he looked as her canine teeth sprouted, grinding their way further and further out of her gums as her jaw snapped open wider than it should have. At the same time, Rebecca's skin seemed to tighten around her head, turning her beautiful face into a skull mask. Matt was reminded of a vulture's bare head in a brief flash of clarity. The two small tears on his cheeks were silently joined by many more.

Almost as soon as the startling transformation happened, it was over. Features slid back into place with surprising speed and again it was lovely Rebecca looking down at him sadly. She softly wiped the tears from his face and spoke.

"It's been happening too quickly to sink in, I know," She soothed. "That's why we have to drive it in deep like this. Hard and fast. Each lesson is going to have to be one you never forget, because you'll only get one try.

She remained astride him as she spoke, letting her words absorb in silence afterward. She had just been a monster, a thing of nightmare and late-night television, but Matt couldn't help but feel uncomfortable and shy as she lingered on his hips. She nodded and reached behind him to unlock his handcuffs before standing.

"At this point we go down to the gym. Most initiates don't really get breakfast, but there's a protein bar in the hall for you. You'll need it. Rita will meet you at the elevator after you change."

With that she was gone. The woman called Rita gave him a last piercing stare, took one step out of the door, and closed it.

It was going to be a long day.

***

How long had it been? An hour? A day? A week? It was hard to say for certain. The hallways all blended together. It might even be the same dank passageway, stretching endlessly into the darkness ahead.

It was hard to tell how far you had been crawling when you could only pull yourself along by your arms.

Red grunted and hauled himself forward another six inches, straining as he lurched over his elbow to plant his face once more into the grimy concrete. His cheekbones were bruised and he heard a muffled *crack* as he chipped a tooth. Exhausted, he lay there for a time.

After the man (was it really a man?) had broken his spine, Red had been abandoned in that god-awful building. Lost to consciousness, he had awoken either hours or days later. The first thing he had felt was the pain. Great tidal waves of pain washed over him, all of his shock and adrenaline spent. It was merely a part of his reality now, a raw and pulsing agony that came as naturally as breathing.

After a time he was able to pierce through the pain and form whole thoughts again, fighting his way back to awareness. He was a fighter, born and bred. He had fought his way from the alphabet avenues of the inner city to the elite Marine recon in the Middle East and beyond. He fought his dishonorable discharge and never stopped. There was another appeal form back home waiting for him.

He knew he was supposed to die in this stupid building. Red could hear them in the distance, through the vents and the vibrations in the floor. It was a miracle he hadn't bled out and it was a miracle they hadn't come back to dispose of his body. After several tours of duty, Red was conditioned to accept grim miracles like these and to act on them.

His SERE training was mostly useless in his present condition and location, but he had been able to keep out of sight so far. He retched dizzily as he pulled himself over his left hand now and hit his head on the floor again on the way down. Lights swam in his vision as the cold floor gave him its hard kiss. Red blinked his eyes, but the lights still danced one the floor.

As he gave in to another wave of exhaustion and pain, he gave up on clearing the lights from his vision and accepted it as another fact of his existence. His dizziness passed and he looked up to move forward again.

And saw the window.

***

To Be Continued...

ABOUT THE AUTHOR

Brian Grossman

Brian Grossman is a lover of fiction of all kinds. Born and raised in upstate NY, he studied psychology, religion & philosophy, social work, and jiu jitsu. His hobby, which he is passionate about, is finding and investing in new hobbies. He currently lives  in Florida with his wife, daughter, and 2 loving cats.

BOOKS BY THIS AUTHOR

Short Story

A casual drink at a cozy establishment, or a misstep into a den of thieves? One man is about to find out.

A Pirate Story

The high seas are unforgiving when a ship has a run-in with pirates. Will the crew be able to pull together and survive?

A Brush With Evil

A traveling priest is asked to counsel a couple in need. But with dark forces conspiring, he may be unprepared for what comes next...

Code Trinity

The thrilling tale of a warrior who journeys through exploitation, insurrection, and retribution.

www.ingramcontent.com/pod-product-compliance
Lightning Source LLC
Chambersburg PA
CBHW060918130726
48001CB00006B/2302